Butterfly Meadow

Dazzle's First Day

Look out for other BUTTERFLY MEADOW books:

Twinkle Dives In

Mallow's Top Team

Skipper to the Rescue

Butterfly Meadow

Dazzle's First Day

Olivia Moss

Illustrated by Sam Chaffey

SCHOLASTIC

With special thanks to Narinder Dhami

First published in the UK in 2008 by Scholastic Children's Books
An imprint of Scholastic Ltd
Euston House, 24 Eversholt Street
London, NW1 1DB, UK
Registered office: Westfield Road, Southam, Warwickshire, CV47 0RA
SCHOLASTIC and associated logos are trademarks and / or registered
trademarks of Scholastic Inc.
Series created by Working Partners Ltd

Text copyright © Working Partners, 2008
Illustration copyright © Sam Chaffey, 2008

The moral right of the author
and illustrator of this work has been asserted by them.

Cover illustration © Sam Chaffey 2008

ISBN 978 1 407 10654 0

Printed by
CPI Bookmarque, Croydon
Papers used by Scholastic Children's Books are made from
wood grown in sustainable forests.

1 3 5 7 9 10 8 6 4 2

www.scholastic.co.uk / zone

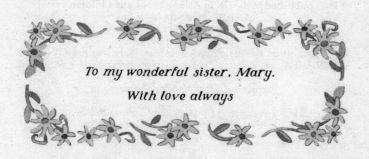

To my wonderful sister, Mary.

With love always

CONTENTS

CHAPTER ONE

The Brand~New Butterfly

"It's time to go," Dazzle said to herself. "Oh, I'm so excited!"

She wiggled inside her tiny home. Slowly the hard shell of the cocoon around her began to crack. It was dark inside the cocoon, but as it split open, rays of sunshine sneaked in, warming her. Dazzle longed to escape.

Just a little more! she

1

thought, turning this way and that.

The cocoon burst wide open. Dazzle wriggled out and perched unsteadily on a nearby leaf. She felt all crumpled after her long sleep. Carefully, she spread her brand-new papery wings in the sunshine.

"Hey, I'm *yellow*!" Dazzle said, admiring her outstretched wings. "I'm a yellow butterfly."

Dazzle blinked at all the bright colours around her. After being inside the tiny,

dark cocoon for so long, this new world looked amazing. Above Dazzle was the blue sky, and below her was a green field, the grass starred with tiny white and yellow flowers. A narrow stream ran along one side of the field.

That water looks lovely, Dazzle thought, batting her wings slowly back and forth. *I wonder who lives there?*

Dazzle had so much to learn. She fluttered her wings backwards and forwards more quickly. It felt good to stretch out. Maybe it was time for a trip. . .

Feeling nervous, Dazzle moved to the edge of the leaf.

"It's a long way down to the ground," she murmured to herself. "But here goes!"

Dazzle launched herself off the leaf. She hung in mid-air, her wings beating frantically. For a second Dazzle felt herself falling through the air, and she gave a little cry of fear as she landed with a bump on the leaf. She rested for a second, then tried

again. This time she only managed to bounce a little. She wouldn't give up. She flapped her wings with slow, long strokes.

She was hovering in the air. She beat her wings faster and faster and soared towards the sky.

"I did it!" Dazzle cried happily. "I'm flying!"

She felt free, fluttering through the warm air. Dazzle dipped down to the ground again but realized that she was heading straight for a tree.

"Oh, no!" Dazzle gasped.

Dazzle flapped her wings faster, but she didn't know what to do. She tried to twist to the side, but that made her wings wobble. She swerved sharply as the tree loomed ahead of her. She managed to dart out of the way at the last minute.

This flying game is more difficult than it looks, Dazzle thought.

Dazzle looked around to see if anyone had seen her mistake, but she couldn't see another animal or insect. "Am I the only butterfly here?" she asked herself.

Dazzle flew on more slowly. As she floated down near the ground, she saw something. A tiny insect, much smaller than Dazzle, was marching up the stem of a plant. Behind the insect were three smaller ones. They all looked exactly alike, with bright-red coats dotted with

black spots. Dazzle wasn't alone after all.

"Hello!" Dazzle called, hovering above them. "I'm a butterfly. What are *you*?"

"We're ladybirds," the biggest insect called back.

"Ladybirds," Dazzle repeated. "You're pretty. Do you walk everywhere, or can you fly like me?"

"Of course we can fly," said one of the smaller insects. "Our mum taught us how. Look!"

All four ladybirds rose up into the air and hovered around Dazzle.

"What's a mum?" Dazzle asked.

"I'm a mum, and these are my babies," said the biggest ladybird. "I brought them into the world and take care of them until they grow up."

"Where's *your* mum?" asked one of the ladybird children.

"I don't know," Dazzle replied.

Dazzle couldn't help feeling sad. Where was her mum?

"Well, look after yourself," said the mother ladybird. "Come along, kids. Let's go and find some tasty greenfly for lunch."

The ladybirds flew away, leaving Dazzle behind.

CHAPTER TWO

Blackbird Attack!

Dazzle fluttered over to a clump of trees in a corner of the field. Suddenly she heard a loud flapping behind her. Her wings were getting knocked about by a sudden breeze. Dazzle spun round.

A blackbird was swooping down towards her, his yellow beak open, ready to gobble her up! Dazzle gasped with fright as the blackbird made a grab for her, snapping his beak. She managed to dart out of the way, flying as quickly as she could past a tree

and zigzagging between the green leaves.

Everything went quiet. Dazzle couldn't hear the flapping of the blackbird's wings behind her any longer. With a sigh of relief, she decided that he had given up and gone away. But as she fluttered out from behind a large leaf, the blackbird flew straight at her.

"Help!" Dazzle gasped. The big bird was so close that Dazzle could see his wide-open beak and the red of his mouth as he snapped at her again.

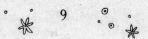

9

Dazzle ducked behind a branch. The blackbird followed close behind, his bright eyes fixed on her as she raced to the tree top.

"Help!" Dazzle cried as the blackbird caught up with her. She could feel her heart fluttering. But she had to be brave. With one quick flick of her wings, she turned in a circle and flew in the opposite direction.

"I didn't even know I could change direction that quickly," Dazzle panted. "Oh no, the blackbird's coming after me again!"

The blackbird looked angry as he

zoomed towards Dazzle. She flew as quickly as she could. Maybe she could go faster than the blackbird and get away.

Dazzle's wings beat so fast that her muscles ached. She darted across the field. Again she thought the blackbird had given up. But then she heard the terrible *flap-flap-flap* of his wings close behind her.

"The blackbird's catching up!" Dazzle cried. "Oh, it's not fair. I *can't* be eaten so soon after coming out of my cocoon."

"Over here!" a small voice called. "Follow me!"

For a moment Dazzle thought she was imagining things. Then a small, pale-blue butterfly skittered through the air nearby. Dazzle stared at her in amazement. Another butterfly!

"This way!" the butterfly called, swooping towards the hedge at the front of the field.

Dazzle followed her. The two butterflies zoomed across the field, their wings a colourful blur. Dazzle hadn't even realized that she could fly so fast! She was so close that the little butterfly's wings tickled her nose. Dazzle didn't dare look back, but she knew the blackbird was behind them. How would they *both* escape from the hungry bird?

The hedge was full of wildflowers, but the blue butterfly headed straight for a big plant covered with pink blooms. She darted inside the twisting stems of the plant, and Dazzle followed.

"Mind your wings," the butterfly told Dazzle. "These thorns are very sharp."

Dazzle noticed the plant stems were covered with small, sharp needles.

"This is a rambling rose," the blue butterfly added as they landed on a leaf in the middle of the hedge. "No bird can get past *these* thorns!"

The blackbird hovered just beside the hedge, peering through the tangle. With a squawk, he flew off.

Dazzle was saved!

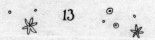

CHAPTER THREE

A New Friend

"Oh, thank you!" Dazzle gasped. "I've only come out of my cocoon today, and I didn't want to get eaten."

"Just remember to look for a rambling rose if you want to escape from hungry birds in the future," the other butterfly told her. She flew to the front of the hedge and peered out. "The blackbird's gone. Shall we go and get a drink of nectar? You must be thirsty after all that excitement."

"Oh yes please," Dazzle said.

The blue butterfly fluttered neatly

between the thorny stems and out of the hedge again. As Dazzle followed, she thought the butterfly's wings were beautiful. They shone bright blue in the sunshine.

"Come on, I'll take you to my favourite flower," Dazzle's new friend told her.

The two butterflies zoomed along the hedge. Dazzle could see that the little blue butterfly was *much* better at flying than she was. She could spin and turn and skim over the tops of leaves, hardly touching them at all. Dazzle decided that she'd have to practise a lot to be as good as *that*. Maybe the blue butterfly would help her.

"Here we are!" The blue butterfly hovered above a sweet-scented climbing plant. It was covered with creamy-yellow flowers tipped with pink. "This is called a honeysuckle." She unfurled her long narrow tongue, dipped it into one of the flowers and took a long drink. "Try it," she said, twirling happily around Dazzle. "It's lovely."

Dazzle lowered her head inside a flower. She took a sip of the sweet nectar.

"Oh, it *is* lovely," she sighed, and had another sip, then another.

A loud buzzing noise behind her made Dazzle jump. She looked around and saw a yellow and black insect flying lazily through the honeysuckle flowers.

"Don't be scared," said the blue butterfly. "It's a bumblebee. They're friendly."

"Hello there," called the bee. He took a sip of nectar and then flew over to them. "This honeysuckle's nice, isn't it? Have you tried the daisies over there?"

"No, we haven't," the blue butterfly replied. Dazzle was too shy to say anything. "Is the nectar good?"

"Delicious!" the bee buzzed.

"The cornflowers are lovely this year, too," the blue butterfly said. "Have you tasted them?"

"Not yet," said the bee. "I'll do that right now!" He floated off towards a clump of bright-blue flowers.

"Come on," the butterfly said to Dazzle. "Let's go and try the daisies."

Dazzle flew after her new friend towards a patch of white flowers with bright-yellow centres.

"You know what?" said the blue butterfly, landing on one of the daisies. "You haven't told me your name yet."

"You haven't told me yours either," Dazzle said, laughing. "I'm Dazzle."

"And my name is Skipper," said the butterfly, taking a sip of nectar. "I'm a Holly Blue."

Dazzle looked puzzled as she took a drink too. "I thought you said your name was Skipper?"

Skipper nodded. "It is," she replied. "But Holly Blue is the *kind* of butterfly I am. What kind of butterfly are you?"

"I don't know." Dazzle glanced round at her wings. "I'm just a yellow butterfly."

"No one is *just* a butterfly!" Skipper declared. "Every butterfly has a name for the type of butterfly they are."

"So what am I called then?" asked Dazzle.

"I don't know," Skipper said. "But we can find out."

"How?" Dazzle asked.

Skipper was flitting around her, looking excited.

"There's a big meadow not far from here," she explained. "*All* the butterflies go there. We have a great time. Sometimes the air is so full of butterflies, you can hardly see the sky."

"It sounds wonderful," said Dazzle. She couldn't wait to see it. Maybe her mummy might be there.

"It is," Skipper agreed. "And I've seen other butterflies there who are just like you, Dazzle!"

"Like *me*?" Dazzle asked. "You mean *yellow* butterflies?"

"Yes," Skipper told her, "and they'll be able to tell you what kind of butterfly you are!"

"Oh, I'd love to go there," Dazzle sighed. "Could you tell me the way to get to the meadow, Skipper?"

"I'll take you there myself," Skipper said.

Dazzle was so happy she whirled up into the air. She was going to meet other yellow butterflies and find out exactly what kind of butterfly she was.

CHAPTER FOUR

Dazzle's Journey

"Follow me, Dazzle." Skipper darted across the hedge, dancing through the sunbeams. "Let's go to Butterfly Meadow."

Dazzle followed her new friend. They flew into the field on the other side of the hedge. The field was full of enormous, strange-looking animals. They didn't have wings but did have large furry heads, big eyes and long tails that swished back and forth.

"Oh, what are *those*?" Dazzle gasped, feeling a tiny bit scared. "They're so big."

One of the animals turned its head and said *Moo!*

"They're called cows," Skipper explained. "Don't worry, they're gentle."

"I didn't know there were so many other animals," Dazzle remarked as they fluttered past. "Now I've met ladybirds and cows."

"Well, butterflies are best, of course!" Skipper said. "But there are lots of other lovely animals. Come and see!"

Skipper led Dazzle over to a patch of tall grass underneath a tree.

"Can you see anything down there?" asked Skipper as they landed on a large leaf.

Dazzle was puzzled. "No, I can't see *anything*—" she began. Then she spotted a cosy nest of leaves right in the middle of the grass. Inside the nest was an animal with brown spikes, curled into a tight ball. Three tiny, spiky babies were fast asleep, cuddled up close to their mother.

"Oh, aren't they lovely?" Dazzle asked. "What are they?"

"They're called hedgehogs," Skipper explained.

"Do you think we ought to wake them up?" Dazzle said. "It's *such* a lovely day, and they're missing all the sunshine!"

"Hedgehogs always sleep in the daytime," Skipper told her, fluttering off again. "They come out at night to feed."

Taking a last look at the sleeping hedgehogs, Dazzle flew after Skipper. There was a lot to learn. Dazzle had never dreamt that this world would be such an interesting place. Before she was a butterfly, she was tucked up in her cosy cocoon. She'd only seen faint colours and heard muffled sounds while she was inside. Now everything was bright and beautiful.

The two butterflies flew on. Along the way Skipper showed Dazzle the spiders' webs strung along the hedges. They spiralled outwards in lots of tiny rows which caught the summer sunlight and glittered like silver.

"Look, Dazzle!" Skipper called out. She pointed at the honeybees buzzing around the wildflowers and the dragonflies skimming the surface of the stream. They flew through a pretty little wood full of bluebells and then out of the cool shade of the trees into the sunlight again.

"We're nearly there, Dazzle!" Skipper said, sounding excited. "There's the meadow, across the next hedge!"

Dazzle could see a lush green meadow dotted with tall feathery grasses which swayed in the breeze. The air was full of colours and hundreds of butterflies! Dazzle could see deep red and emerald green, pale blue and gleaming white, purple and orange and brown.

"The meadow's full of butterflies!" Dazzle cried.

"I told you," said Skipper, flying ahead.

Dazzle watched her friend dart over the hedge into Butterfly Meadow. She felt nervous for a moment. There were a lot of new butterflies to meet here.

"Am I ready for this?" she whispered.

CHAPTER FIVE

Butterfly Friends

The butterflies criss-crossed the meadow. They dipped down to the grasses, nearly touching the seed-heads.

Dazzle had no idea that there were so many different butterflies in the world. Some were bigger than Dazzle, while others were much smaller.

"Oh, Skipper," Dazzle gasped, hurrying to catch her friend up. "This meadow *is* a special place. I hope I find some other yellow butterflies, like me."

"Let's go and see." Skipper skimmed across the grass, and Dazzle followed her.

Maybe I will find my mum here, Dazzle thought. But even if she didn't, she *wasn't* alone in the world. There were hundreds of other butterflies!

Skipper was flying straight for a large plant in the middle of the meadow. The plant was covered with lavender-coloured flowers. All the butterflies were gathering there.

"Hi, Mallow!" Skipper said to a small white butterfly. "Hello, Spot! How are you?"

"Hello," Spot, a red and black butterfly, called back. "Your wings look really pretty today." She stared at Dazzle as she passed by.

Skipper landed and settled herself on a leaf. Dazzle dipped down to join her, feeling shy as all the other butterflies looked at them.

"This is Dazzle," said Skipper. "She came out of her cocoon today."

"Well done!" some of the butterflies called. "Pleased to meet you."

"Thank you," said Dazzle.

"Dazzle doesn't know what kind of butterfly she is," Skipper went on. "Can anyone help her, please?"

Dazzle looked hopefully at the other butterflies. They fluttered around her, inspecting her markings.

"I know exactly what Dazzle is," Mallow said at last. "She's a Pale Clouded Yellow!"

"Oh, yes," the other butterflies agreed. "Definitely a Pale Clouded Yellow."

"A Pale Clouded Yellow," Dazzle said to herself. "That sounds lovely." She looked at the other butterflies. "But where's my mum?"

The butterflies glanced at each other.

"Dazzle, you don't have a mum," Spot explained. "You came from a cocoon. We all did."

"But the baby ladybirds had a mum," said Dazzle.

"Ladybirds are different," Mallow replied. "Butterflies are *special*."

"Another butterfly cared enough to lay the egg that made you, Dazzle," Spot said. "But after that, it was up to you to bring yourself into the world on your own."

"And you did, Dazzle," Skipper pointed out. "You managed to wriggle out of your cocoon all by yourself. You're a very clever butterfly!"

"Yes, very clever!" the other butterflies agreed, fluttering around

Dazzle. Dazzle slowly opened and closed her wings. She felt proud of herself. She *was* a clever butterfly! And now, with so many butterfly friends, she would never feel alone.

CHAPTER SIX

Feeling Shy

"You know, we haven't seen a Pale Clouded Yellow like Dazzle here for a while," Mallow announced. "We must have a party tonight to welcome Dazzle to Butterfly Meadow!"

"Mallow loves organizing things," Skipper whispered to Dazzle. "We'll have a wonderful party."

But Dazzle didn't understand. "What's a party?" she asked.

"A party means having a great time," Skipper explained. "And butterfly parties are always fun!"

"Look, the sun's setting," called Mallow. "Let's fly round the meadow and invite everyone to the party."

The butterflies all rose into the air like a huge, colourful cloud. Then they flew off in all directions. Dazzle glanced at the sky. The blue was now streaked with pink and gold and the sun was slowly sinking out of sight.

"Come on, Dazzle," Skipper called. "We'll go and find some friends and ask them if they want to come to our party."

"But I don't know anyone," Dazzle replied.

"Well, you soon will," Skipper laughed. She floated down towards the ground and perched on the petals of a blue flower. Dazzle flew down to join her.

"Hello!" Skipper said cheerfully to a spider who was spinning a glistening web between two tall blades of grass at the edge of the meadow. "We're having a party tonight. Will you come?"

"Oh, yes, please," the spider replied. "Can I bring my family?"

"Of course," Skipper said. "The party's for my friend Dazzle. She's just found out she's a Pale Clouded Yellow."

"See?" Skipper fluttered around Dazzle as the spider continued spinning. "Everyone's friendly. Now you invite someone."

Dazzle looked around. She saw a large bee dipping in and out of some purple bell-shaped flowers close by.

"Hello," she called uncertainly.

The bee was buzzing so loudly that he didn't hear her.

"Hello there!" Dazzle said again.

The bee popped out of one of the flowers and buzzed over to Dazzle. He was covered in dusty yellow pollen. Dazzle realized that it was the same bee she and Skipper had met earlier at the honeysuckle plant.

"Oh, hello again," the bee said.

"I was wondering if you'd like to come to the butterflies' party tonight," Dazzle asked.

"A party?" The bee sounded excited. "Try and keep me away! I love parties!" He buzzed round the two butterflies.

"We'll see you later then," Dazzle said with a laugh. As the bee dived into another flower, she turned to Skipper. "You were right, Skipper. Everyone is friendly."

Dazzle didn't need to feel shy any more. And tonight she was going to her first party!

CHAPTER SEVEN

Party Time!

Dazzle was beginning to feel more at home as she and Skipper flew around the meadow. They invited everyone they saw to the party. As the sun set, the guests began to arrive.

"What happened to the sun?" asked Dazzle, as it grew darker. A large pale circle appeared in the sky.

"Don't worry," said Skipper. "It'll be back tomorrow. The moon isn't as bright, but our special guests will light up the evening. Look!"

Dazzle saw some little brown insects

with large eyes crawling through the grass towards them. Three stripes on their bodies glowed yellow-green. They shone in the darkness, lighting up the meadow with polka dots of light.

"Hello, butterflies," called the insect at the front of the line. "We're really looking forward to the party."

"They're called glow-worms," Skipper explained.

"How clever," Dazzle said. "Now we can see everything."

"This way," called Skipper, leading the guests towards one of the hedges. "The best nectar is over here."

The butterflies and their guests gathered around the hedge to sip nectar together. Dazzle joined in. As she was sipping from a honeysuckle blossom, she heard music coming from overhead. She looked up. A group of brown birds sat in a nearby tree, singing loudly.

"Those birds are nightingales," said Mallow, who was sipping from the same blossom. "They always sing at our parties. They have the sweetest voices of all the birds in the meadow."

As the nightingales' song grew louder, the butterflies began fluttering up into the air.

"Come on, Dazzle," called Skipper. "This is going to be fun."

Dazzle followed her friend. The butterflies swooped and soared, whirling and turning, rising and falling. Dazzle

watched her friends as Skipper flew circles above her head. Mallow bobbed up and down, and Spot flitted from side to side.

"We love dancing like this," said Skipper. "You try, Dazzle!"

"Yes, Dazzle!" sang the nightingales. "Let's see you dance!"

Dazzle launched herself into the cloud of butterflies. Her wings were trembling.

"Oh!" she gasped as she almost flew straight into a small brown butterfly. "Sorry!"

"Don't worry about it," said the brown butterfly cheerfully.

But Dazzle felt embarrassed. She turned quickly to the left and almost bumped wings with a big yellow and black butterfly.

"Sorry," she
said again.

"It's OK," the
butterfly replied. "We
were all beginners once."
The butterflies began moving
away from Dazzle to give her more

room. But Dazzle felt silly dancing by herself. She fluttered further away from the glow-worms' light, into the dark edges of the meadow.

I'll never be as good at flying as these butterflies are, Dazzle thought.

CHAPTER EIGHT

Dazzle's Big Dance

Suddenly Skipper appeared beside Dazzle.

"Stay close to me, Dazzle," Skipper called. "Now, fly to the left."

Dazzle did as Skipper said.

"And now to the right," Skipper told her. "Fly up high with me and then we swoop back down again, like this."

Dazzle was still nervous and her wings were trembling so much that she couldn't fly very fast. But it was easier now that she and Skipper were away from the other butterflies. She stuck close to Skipper.

"Go right," Skipper called. "Now, left. Down and then up."

Dazzle realized that the dance wasn't so difficult after all. Her wings stopped shaking and she began to enjoy herself.

"Look at me, Skipper!" Dazzle called happily as she fluttered up and down. "I can do it!"

"Come on then," Skipper called back. "Let's join the others."

Dazzle danced into the middle of the cloud of butterflies. She swirled and swooped, skimming over the tops of grasses and soaring up towards the white moon. This time she didn't bump into a single butterfly.

"Wow! Look at Dazzle," said Spot. "She's a wonderful dancer."

"Go, Dazzle!" called the other butterflies. Everyone cheered.

Dazzle soared higher, feeling as though her heart would burst with happiness.

Finally it was time for the party to end. All the guests said goodnight and set off for home. The glow-worms helped them

see where they were going. Tired but happy, Dazzle floated down to the ground behind Skipper. *What a day*, Dazzle thought sleepily. It was difficult to believe that she'd only come out of her cocoon that morning. So much had happened since then.

"Come on," said Skipper. "I'll show you the cosy place where I always sleep."

She led Dazzle over to the tall plant in the middle of the meadow. There the two

butterflies tucked themselves underneath one of the large leaves, folding back their wings.

"I hope you enjoyed your first day out of your cocoon, Dazzle," said Skipper.

"Oh, I did!" Dazzle replied. "Thanks to you, Skipper. I hope we'll always be friends."

"Me too," Skipper said. "Goodnight, Dazzle."

"Goodnight," said Dazzle.

I'm so lucky, Dazzle thought. She'd met Skipper and lots of other butterflies.

Dazzle felt herself getting sleepier as the glow-worms' lights went out, one by one, in Butterfly Meadow. Dazzle's first day as a butterfly had been a real adventure. She was sure even more adventures would happen tomorrow.

"Welcome to Butterfly Meadow, Dazzle," Skipper whispered.

"Thanks, Skipper," Dazzle replied.

She closed her eyes.

Dazzle was home.

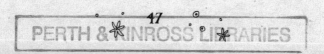

Read about more adventures in
Butterfly Meadow

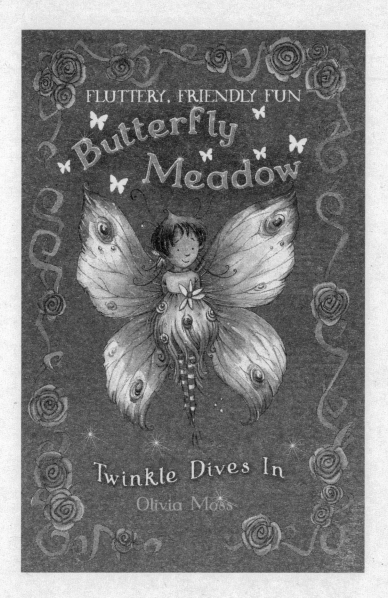

FLUTTERY, FRIENDLY FUN

Butterfly Meadow

Twinkle Dives In

Olivia Moss

FLUTTERY, FRIENDLY FUN

Butterfly Meadow

Mallow's Top Team

Olivia Moss

FLUTTERY, FRIENDLY FUN

Butterfly Meadow

Skipper to the Rescue

Olivia Moss